A CLANDESTINE MYSTERY

A Dr. Kaili Worthy Series

By Kay A. Oliver

"Somewhere, something incredible is waiting to be known."
— **Carl Sagan**

"No great discovery was ever made without a bold guess."
— **Isaac Newton**

DEDICATION

A feeling of being blessed hits me every morning I awake. There are people in my life who support me, make me laugh, and that make life worth living. Being surrounded by these people, either near or far, we keep in touch and hopefully brighten each other's lives.

It is to those people I dedicate this book.

Kaili Worthy Series by Kay A. Oliver

The Edgewater Nile - Book 1
Hidden Fears and Secrets – Book 2
A Clandestine Mystery - Book 3
Buried Together - Book 4
Death To A Lie - Book 5

Copyright © 2020 Kay A. Oliver. All Rights Reserved.

This is a work of fiction. Names, characters, places and incidents either are the product of the author's imagination, or are used factitiously, and any resemblance to actual persons, living or dead, business establishments, events, or locales is entirely coincidental.

AUTHOR'S NOTE

Though these books are about a strong independent woman who loves her career in archaeology, they also examine two things. One, is an equal and healthy relationship with her husband. And two, more importantly how we view souls.

Here in America, and many parts of the world, modern day graveyards and burial sites are revered. If a team of people came into a graveyard and began to unearth all the remains, the community would be in an uproar.

With that said, it seems we are all okay with unearthing burial sites from ancient times, one after another, and placing mummies on exhibit.

These books are fictional. The book does raise the question if we should reveal all within these tombs or leave many where they were buried.

PROLOGUE

It has been a whirlwind several months for Dr. Kaili Worthy. All starting from the simple decision to review and research artifacts already at the Nile Egyptian Museum in Fremont, California leading to a discovery of her career. The first of several to come.

Finding a skeleton set of bones that had been on sale in the black market, Dr. Kaili Worthy started to research their origins. In doing so, she thought they had a value more important than many believed.

Kaili began by pulling the bones out of storage and examining them. Due to the verbal history floating with the skeleton, it appeared to come from an area in Egypt that could be a location for Queen Cleopatra.

Deciding to complete a DNA sample, Dr Kaili confirmed the skeleton to be that of Cleopatra Selene, the Queen's daughter. What happened next surprised Kaili beyond belief. Someone started writing in Hierographic Cartouches using the skeleton to form designs and images in the sand on a table.

Suddenly it made sense. Selene's essence, or some would say soul, was with her bones and could communicate with Kaili.

But the museum also had the Mummy of Sethos I, also known as Seti, in the other room.

Kaili began to realize that the preparation for burial during the times of the pharaohs actually did in fact tie them to their remains. Selene was not the only one there. Seti's soul or spirit was also in the room with them.

Communication was not an easy flow of information as Seti, having been at the museum a lot longer than Selene, had picked up only a little bit of English. However, Kaili's studies had included learning the Egyptian language. Together they told a story of being at the Palace of the Gods after their deaths. That is until their tombs were discovered and excavated. Eventually they found themselves at the museum where their remains were being stored.

Kaili's discovery of Cleopatra Selene had ignited a new interest in archaeology and took Kaili Worthy on a worldwide tour of TV and Press interviews.

What no one knew outside of two other people is that Kaili had discovered the ability to communicate with the spirits of Selene and Seti. Kaili knew that divulging this type of information would not be received well in the scientific community without more clear-cut proof and evidence.

- - - -

While Kaili was on her press tour her husband, Derek, solved a case for the F.B.I. of a local murder that essentially ended up concluding a serial killing spree across the US. This brought Police Chief Derek Worthy his own fame.

1

MODERN DAY
NILE EGYPTIAN MUSEUM, FREMONT, CA

Waiting for her friend Doris to visit her and attend the upcoming Museum fundraiser, Kaili became an instructor of the English language to Selene and Seti for the past six weeks. They spent early morning and evening hours on a daily basis to improve their ability to communicate to each other. These were precious times when Kaili's co-workers were not at their stations, when she had the office area to herself.

They were progressing slowly but finding easier ways to speak to one another.

Every day Kaili, Selene and Seti would go out farther and farther to test their distance capabilities. In the past several weeks Kaili had figured out as long as she has something from their body with her, like a toe or finger part, they could travel as far as they wanted to go. And even though Seti and Selene have also practiced picking up light-weight objects, the problem is the object would appear to float to anyone else seeing it. Therefore, Seti and Selene had not figured out a way to carry their own body part themselves to travel on their own. They needed Kaili. Kaili didn't know it yet, but she needed them too.

Kaili knew the Fundraiser was just around the corner and that Dr. Doris Wolf would be in town that day. Fundraisers really weren't Kaili's thing. Politics, asking for money, dressing up like a doll was literally all the things she disliked about her job.

Making matters even more interesting is the fact that the Board of Directors at the museum honored Dr. Kaili Worthy with a promotion to Senior Director of Egyptian Studies with her own office. Of course, it came on the heels of her fame and the new founded recognition of the Museum. It always helps to have a higher title when asking for financial support from others.

This new arrangement would let Kaili perform even more experiments in private, which was a great thing for her.

2

THE WORTHY HOME
COYOTE CREEK AREA OF SAN JOSE
COUNTY, CA

Derek felt like he had been running ragged for the last couple of months due to the recent murder case. With any murder case, Derek always finds himself unable to unwind until the case is solved. Every minute of each day could yield information to unravel the how, why and who of a case. He is desperately aware of the family in mourning and knows every moment longer adds to the pain they feel.

Solving the recent murder of Dr. Sheila Barkley which eventually lead to the discovery of a serial killer, took its toll on Derek and his team. As with all police staff, they often find themselves shorthanded. Derek left it up to Shanice, his Deputy Chief, to ensure each officer got some additional time off to recoup from the busy days. Their mental health was as important as them maintaining their skills.

In taking his own suggestion Derek promised himself some down-time doing something very mind-numbing. Leaving the office early Derek found himself in the family room in the overstuffed white couch, drinking a beer while watching TV.

Kaili was aware of Derek's plans for the day. And

despite her desire to run home and be with him, she knew he needed his own alone time. Instead, she spent the day moving into her new office. It was only a few steps away from the room she had been working in for the past several years. Making it a little easier once she moved in as she knew that she would probably automatically walk her previous route when coming in to work before realizing she no longer worked in that old room.

The new office was about 10 feet by 12 feet. A genuinely nice size for an office. She has a small bookshelf, and an area to be able to run some tests and use her microscope. The office had a window overseeing the parking lot which also allowed her to see some of the city. The window also had a blinding curtain which would allow her to darken the room as she did some types of research.

For now, the walls were bare. She would have to find some art that would reflect her personality to hang behind her desk and the opposing wall. The floor was a white tile which reminded her of hospital flooring.

Her desk is of medium size with a return. The desk is made of dark wood with a one-inch white laminated top. Her printer sits on the return. Her chair was a high back white leatherette chair with aluminum arms and legs. Kaili took a moment to sit in her chair and adjust it to the right height. Loving the fact that she now has her own office, she felt a little lonely. A few minutes later, Kaili found herself unable to stand it any longer and left to go home to be with Derek.

Arriving home Kaili found Derek watching TV in his favorite sweats. She immediately noticed he was in need of a fresh beer. Dropping her women's leather briefcase by the table in the living room and then deposited her keys going into the key bowl, she walked over to the refrigerator to grab a new beer.

"Hello darling," Kaili quipped. Derek returned the reply and began to get up to give her a kiss. Kicking off her heels, she slid into the couch next to him and handed him his beer.

"Ahh thank you. You miss nothing," he praised her.

The show on the TV caught Kaili's attention. It was a ghost hunting show of some sort. She had never known Derek to watch this type of program.

"What are you watching?"

Derek realized he had never flipped the channel beyond the ghost show even though he had been watching some sports earlier. "Oh, I was watching a college game earlier. I started flipping channels and suddenly I saw some investigator using what they call a spirit box to talk with the dead."

"A what?" Kaili asked.

"A Spirit Box." Derek continued to explain. "It is a device created to pick up EVPs or Electronic Voice Phenomena. Instead of just recording the spirit's voice like a regular EVP recorder, this new device lets the investigator hear the voice live, in real time. It actually registers in the white noise between FM and AM frequencies. These are very high frequencies. It seems it is where most paranormal voices can be picked up."

Kaili looked confused. She wondered when Derek started getting into the paranormal world. Was it because of her recent findings? As she personally questioned why he was on the subject she remained silent, Derek pushed his computer over to her.

It was on a web page for the device. She began to read the details. It was small enough to fit in the palm of the hand. You could walk around with it, wherever you go. It looked like an old transistor radio of sorts. It costs around two-hundred dollars. Her eyes brighten at the thought.

"Are you suggesting I buy one of these to see if Seti or Selene can reach out directly to me?" Derek shook his head yes.

"How could it hurt?"

Right then the show came back on TV after the break. A female paranormal investigator was using a Spirit Box on the show. Kaili became intrigued.

The Investigator started asking questions. "Who is in the room with me?" The device crackled and then a faith voice was heard "…Troy…". "Troy who?" the investigator asked. The voice was heard again but it was hard to make out. "Are you dead?" she asked. He replied "…y..ess..".

The session went on. Kaili knew she would want to try this new device out, but also realized the scientific community had little to no faith in paranormal activities and certainly did not give credit to ghost or paranormal shows.

She immediately reached for the computer. Derek let her know he had completed some research on the device and found the one on the screen was the best recommended one he located. Kaili went ahead and ordered it immediately. She considered having it shipped directly to the house for confidentiality, but since they both worked, she felt her office was the better choice. She also paid for the rush option. The sooner, the better.

3

MODERN DAY
NILE EGYPTIAN MUSEUM, FREMONT, CA

Waiting for the precious package to be delivered over the previous day, Kaili had been trying to communicate to Seti and Selene about the possibility of being able to communicate via their voice. It was very hard to explain to those who lived thousands of years ago how modern technology could work. Kaili felt they had a general idea though they were still confused, but she knew they would be willing to try anything.

Their cooperation since their discovery seemed to be unlimited. Seti and Selene tried genuinely hard to learn English, but of course Kaili did not know how well they could speak the language. She still believed that Seti knew more having been at the museum longer. Over the past few weeks, he had explained how the museum classes held weekly that taught patrons how to read hieroglyphics cartouches let him learn English in reverse.

Unlike Seti, Selene had only been at the museum a few months but appeared to be a very quick study. Kaili was now hoping they had learned enough to start communicating by speaking to each other.

As she opened her office door, there sitting on her desk was a package. She was excited. Taking off her coat, putting her purse in her desk drawer, Kaili grabbed her letter opener and exposed the package contents. It was the

Spirit Box. Taking it out of the carton, Kaili hid the device in her top drawer. She didn't want someone to walk in and see the device on her desk as she studied the product instructions.

Fully understanding how to work with the device, Kaili got up quickly and locked her office door. She drew the shade down to make it look as if she was not in. Returning to her desk, she pulled the items out of her drawer. She placed the batteries into the small black box and plugged in the mic.

"Selene or Seti... are either of you here?" Kaili invited. The small table against the wall with the magnifying lamp moved a little. She remembered there was sand on the table. Someone was answering her.

"No... Don't use the sand. Please ... use your voice. Speak to me. Tell me if you are here."

The box sizzled and cracked a couple of times. Then she heard a man's voice "...here...".

Kaili became overwhelmed. It was working. Before she could ask the next question, she heard a female voice" ...Her...e." That must be Selene. It was astonishing. Another silent break through. Would she tell Doris? She was due to arrive at the fundraiser that evening, and this would all new to her. You never know how someone is going to react with news like this.

Deciding it might be better to see Doris' initial reaction about the essence of pharaohs staying with their bodies the following day. It would be too much to take in on one evening. Kaili knew it was going to be news that would need more time to explain than just a late-night reveal.

    She would have to wait.

4

LATER THE EVENING
NILE EGYPTIAN MUSEUM, FREMONT, CA

The fear was mounting in her gut as Kaili knew she would be sharing her full discovery, without mentioning the ability to communicate with the Egyptian souls, in the next several hours. Yet she had to maintain her composure while greeting guests at the evening fundraiser.

Looking dazzling, Kaili decided to wear her full-length floral print dress in light pinks and lavenders. A silver sequin 3-inch band wrapped around her small waist and flutter elbow length sleeves which she loved. Her hair was pulled back in a French bun with ringlets of her dark hair framing her face.

Derek was in attendance with her wearing his black evening tux and a matching silver cummerbund. He almost looked like the character 007.

The evening event was being held in the largest hall in the Museum that just happened to house Seti's mummy. That fact did not leave Kaili's mind.

All of the Museum's Executives were in attendance along with local politicians. Several wealthy millionaires were in attendance as well as the press. Kaili was the star attraction and Selene's skeleton had been brought in and prepared as an exhibit. Kaili had to return the bones she had been using for the meantime but decided she would have the lab create some duplicates so that they could be swapped out and kept on hand for further study. Afterall, the precedent was set when they did the same for Seti's mummy.

Kaili felt like her eyes were darting everywhere. Anything that seemed to move on its own was in question for her. Was Selene or Seti moving it to let her know they were there or was her mind just playing tricks on her. It was making her feel unsettled. She was thankful that her husband continued to escort her throughout the fundraiser staying at her side the entire time. She had her own bodyguard. Many in attendance knew him anyways since he is the San Jose Police Chief.

Everyone wanted to meet Kaili. The questions were relentless. Many of the same questions about what made her even consider researching the skeleton in storage.

As with every discovery there was a layer of doubters. They were present too. Some had made formal requests to test the DNA themselves, wanting to collect some bone samples to use. This was very concerning to Kaili since she knew it meant more than just removing a bone from the skeleton.

She was thankful that the museum held the stance that releasing any of the skeleton was not an option. And since Kaili had provided a lot of the original sample to the lab for testing, some of the leftover could be shared for further testing. The concerns were low as the Museum had already hired an outside lab to confirm the results before even making a public announcement about the findings.

The room suddenly felt less threatening as Kaili saw Doris enter the room. Dr. Doris Wolf was wearing an electric blue evening gown. The bodice of the dress was flowery applicates with areas that appeared to be see-through on the arms. Long sleeves which ended in small ruffles. The dress was backless to the lower back. The full-length gown draped perfectly to the floor. This was also an opportunity for Doris to let her long dark hair down. She wore a complementary blue rhinestone comb in her hair on the right side.

"Sister," Doris greeted Kaili. It was an affectionate term the use for each other. They had been friends from the start of their college years and had kept in touch ever since. Whenever the opportunity was there, they would visit each other. Even though it might be a gap in their visits, it never felt that way. It was like they were together just the day before.

"I'm so glad you are here." Kaili was excited to find out about everything Doris has been working on. "I can't wait to hear more about your Canadian Maiden. What have you found out? So much to catch up on."

Cameras were clicking like crazy. It was as if the paparazzi had entered the room. Two very famous female archaeologist who were both working on major discoveries together in one room. It was a photo op no one could dare miss.

It was time for Kaili to make her presentation and ask for more funding to the Museum. As she entered the stage, Derek winked at her to say 'you've got this.' Kaili literally told the same story she had used on her world press tour a few months earlier. She added some additional highlights since she could reference Selene's skeleton displayed in the room.

The feeling of not being a hundred percent truthful of the full discovery came over Kaili as it usually does but with a little more force. Now she was not telling co-workers or her bosses there was more. There was a lot more.

As she walked off the stage, several people were there to congratulate her. All Kaili wanted was to go home. Her stomach was twisted. Her thoughts were bouncing around in her head afraid she would be found out. Maintaining her serenity on the outside was becoming exhausting.

After a few hours, some people were beginning to leave. Derek knew instantly it was the time to make their escape. Discreetly he rounded up Doris and snuck the three of them out the back door. Derek had conveniently made sure to park in the back for that quick getaway.

5

EARLY MORNING, THE WORTHY HOME COYOTE CREEK AREA OF SAN JOSE COUNTY, CA

As soon as they got home from the evening's event, they could not change their clothes fast enough. Derek carried in Doris's luggage and showed her to her room. It was the room she always stayed in. It was pleasant and had its own bathroom. A double size bed took over the middle of the room with a large white comforter draped over it. It beckons to her. The day had been long.

She unpacked everything since she would be staying for a few days. Right now, the most important item was her comfy P.Js. Removing her make-up and washing up, she was ready for bed in a few quick minutes.

Just before jumping in bed, she heard Kaili and Derek heading back down stairs. She was unsure if they expected her to join them or not. She decided she would.

"You're still up?" Kaili asked Doris.

"Heard you two and thought I'd at least say goodnight."

"Don't let us keep you up. But you are welcome to a night cap."

That sounded perfect. Doris joined them as Derek poured 3 drinks. He already knew Doris preferred a flavored vodka. Kaili had some whiskey, while Derek took it up a notch from his beer and had a brandy.

They all sat in the family room and talked about the night's outcomes. It appeared the Museum had the largest donation record in its history bringing in over one-hundred and twenty thousand dollars.

They had a little fun talking about outfits and fancy head dresses worn by some of theextraordinarily rich. Some of the evening's conversations they found themselves in, made them laugh. Plus, those people who thought the whole discovery was a fraud.

"There are always those who love being a nay-sayer. Not sure what they get out of it," Doris quipped.

Kaili laughed. "Even though the DNA proves it they have to say no."

"Well tomorrow is another day." Derek added and probably hinting it was time to sleep. He was drained.

"I go into the office around 8 am. You willing to go in with me tomorrow Doris?" Kaili asked.

"You bet. If I go to bed now... I think I can get up in time." She giggled.

With that, the three of them placed their drinking glasses on the kitchen counter and headed up to bed. They would all sleep well.

6

NEXT DAY
NILE EGYPTIAN MUSEUM, FREMONT, CA

Kaili and Doris were on their way to the museum. Kaili was driving and enjoying Doris talking about her discoveries with the Canadian Maiden.

"I swear every day we find something new. What I love most is the fact that these finds are frozen in time. Did you know she still had blood in a couple of organs?" Doris stated.

Kaili was excited by that news. "No, I did not. That is astonishing news."

Doris continued. "Based on both tissue samples and the contents of her stomach, she fed on shellfish, salmon and some artic ground squirrel." Thinking for a moment, Doris went on. "She was around 13 to 16 years old. She was wearing beautiful hand sewn boots made from squirrel pellets. What we don't know is how she ended up buried in the ice. It appears she was not there as long as the Canadian Ice Man who many believe was caught in the "little Ice age.""

Pausing a moment before going on, Doris was excited to reveal some news that was not public yet. Kaili could feel Doris's hesitation.

"The DNA tests reveal 14 people who are living who are related to her."

Kaili gasped. She had not thought of running Selene's DNA through a genealogy site. "That is amazing. Have you reached out to them?"

Doris responded. "Yes, we have. They all live either in Canada or just over the border in the states."

Arriving at the Museum parking lot, Kaili turned off the car but had more questions. Before even getting out of the car she asked, "What did they say?"

Doris was eager to let her know. "They were excited to hear about it. We are even going to have a family day at the lab and let them come and meet their relative. The press will have a field day."

With that, they both headed into the museum.

Once in Kaili's office, Kaili was ready to reveal a lot more to Doris. She had made sure her day's schedule was open. No meetings and no calls scheduled. She knew that once she started talking about her unknown discoveries, that they would need time for Doris to take it all in and fully understand what it all meant.

Kaili was nervous. She wasn't sure how Doris would respond to the news. Taking in a deep breath, Kaili started to talk.

Doris could see Kaili's apprehension. She knew whatever she was going to hear next must be something very special.

"Here is a part of Selene's skeleton. And here is a part of Seti's toe."

Doris interjected. "Seti? Sethos I?"

"Yes. We have his mummy in the other room."

"I will want to see that before I leave here."

Kaili smirked a little. "I am 100% sure you will."

Kaili then sprinkled some sand onto the top of her desk as Doris watched and wondered what was happening.

She was ready and nervous as hell. "Good morning," Kaili announced. "Hoping you can help me. Can you say hi?" she asked.

Doris was beginning to think Kaili was going mental. Who was she talking to?

The sand began to move on its own. Doris saw it. An H was forming. Followed by an I. Doris looked at the word and looked back at Kaili with a puzzled look.

The sand began to move again. A W showed up, followed by an H and then an O. Who? Kaili knew immediately that one of them was asking who Doris was.

Kaili replied by introducing Doris as both a great friend and fellow archaeologist. As she started to tell them about the frozen mummy that Doris was working on Doris interrupted. "Hold on. Who the hell are you talking to?"

"You're right. Doris, please meet Selene and Seti."

Doris was frozen. She was trying awfully hard to put this together.

Kaili started to explain it better. She knew she had just dropped a bombshell on her friend.

"What we have discovered, and not released to anyone yet, is the fact that the Egyptian mummies preparation keeps them associated with their remains." She lingered for a moment to let it sink in.

Continuing. "We made this discovery the day we got the DNA results on Selene. Seti had rearranged her skeleton bones in Hieroglyphs which we translated. Seti had learned some English while being here and listening to people speak. But in the last few months I have been trying to teach them more."

Doris was amazed. She was starting to absorb the information.

Remaining quiet for a few moments, Kaili pulled out the spirit box from her desk and turned it on. Kaili asked the next question. "Seti are you here?"

The box crackled and then a low male voice said yes. Kaili continued. "Selene are you here as well?" And again, the box made noise and a female voice a bit stronger said YES.

Doris was staring at Kaili. "They are here," She almost whispered. The spirit box went off again "...yes..."

With reality setting in, Doris was becoming exhilarated. "What does this mean?"

"It means that their essence stays with their bodies. The preparation for burial must adhere their bodies and their spirits together. What I have been told by them is that they felt they were at the Palace of Gods long before someone excavated them."

Doris's eyes darted around as she was looking up toward the ceiling. It was evident she was thinking in super mode. 'There is so much we can learn from them."

Kaili nodded in agreement.

"How have you kept this from Derek?"

"He knows. He was here when we made this discovery."

"Wow. Well, we both know he is good at keeping secrets."

After explaining that the museum executive had not

been informed about this discovery yet. Only one other person knows outside of Derek and herself and she is not talking.

Using the spirit box, Doris and Kaili began to ask a number of questions with Selene and Seti happily replying to the best of their abilities.

7

LATER THAT SAME DAY
NILE EGYPTIAN MUSEUM, FREMONT, CA

The day wore on. Kaili and Doris asked about the pyramids, about customs and practices of the culture. They loved hearing from Selene about her favorite foods. Though they had improved their English over the last couple of months, the communication was still awkward at best.

A few hours had passed and Kaili knew they shouldn't keep pounding answers out of their spiritual guests. Kaili had another question but this time it was for Doris. "We can't tell anybody, can we?"

The mood in the room changed quickly. "No. No, we cannot." Doris was adamant.

"Let's take a break. Thank you Seti and Selene. You have been most helpful. We're going to get something to eat and be right back."

But before they could leave the office, Kaili recognized the fact that Doris's facial expressions would have to change from pure astonishment to normalcy. If that was even possible.

Knowing that bringing up Doris' ex-boyfriend would sour the mood. It was the fastest way to change her attitude. "How is Liam? Seen him lately?"

Doris shot Kaili a look. "Why would you bring him

up? And no."

Smiling Kaili replied, "Because I needed to change that expression on your face before we left the office." Doris laughed.

"Thought you went nuts for a moment."

Still full of questions, Doris carried on as they walked to the museum commissary to grab some food. "Are you aware there are a set of scientists that believe they can re-unite souls with their bodies using DNA? I know it sounds crazy and I have always written them off, but now I wonder if they have had a similar experience and know what we know." Kaili wasn't convinced. She had heard of these theories before. "The problem with their theories is what is their plan to re-ignite the body itself? If you look at Seti's full mummy, it is shriveled, and organs are missing. So, if they are talking about cloning the body then what makes them think they can harness the essence? "

"Let me play devil's advocate. What if you could clone Seti with his DNA? Then ask him if he wants to enter that body. Do you think that would work?"

Kaili couldn't answer fast enough. "No. What is our spirit or essence? Is it part of our DNA? If it is, then your essence would be part of your clone. Right?"

"You are speaking like the results of a transplant? When a person gets a vital organ from someone. Then the recipient starts craving food that the donor loved?"

"Right. There is a lot more to DNA than we know about. And we are not even close to fully understanding." Doris quipped.

Both starving, Kaili and Doris attacked the deli. Each

grabbed their favorite sandwich, some chips, and a drink. Kaili flashed her badge for her discount, and they went at sat at a table away from the others eating there.

Wanting to continue their discussion in private, Doris jumped in. "So, Derek knows. What does he think?"

"I think he wants nothing to do with it. He was never the type to believe in psychics or fortune tellers who reach out to your dead ones. Now it's staring him in the face." Hesitating before going on, Kaili almost didn't want to admit the next part. "We have never spoken about it in detail since that day."

They both sat quiet for a couple of minutes. Finishing up their food they headed back to the office. Doris was contemplating more questions for the two Egyptians. She began to wonder what they were thinking. Are they upset to have been disturbed? They talked so much about the Palace of the Gods. How everyday was perfect. They never aged and never got an illness.

They had spoken about some of the others they had left behind. And they confessed about how they disappeared.

Back in the office, Doris started right in. "Seti. Selene. How do you feel being here? Are you upset your remains were disturbed?"

The spirit box snapped back to life. Seti spoke "rather be back... palace." The room was quiet as everyone expected Selene to speak next but she didn't.

Doris expanded the thought for Seti. "You were happy there. You had made it to your next life and now you were pulled back here. I get it."

Seti voiced his opinion. "Not knowing where or time, rather be with others." His English was still a bit broken. Kaili was proud of what he had learned.

"You are in a country that did not exist in your time. We are across the great ocean. We call it the United States. It is many, many years since you were alive."

Seti had a little idea of where he was due to the large map on the museum wall that pointed out where his tomb was and a *You-are-here* sticker on it that a co-worker placed there previously as a joke.

The room was silent when Selene chimed in. Her English was nowhere near as good as Seti's, but she tried. The spirit box sizzled and then her voice came across, "*...crack... snap...* not...here...alone."

Not sure what Selene was trying to convey, Kaili and Doris thought Selene may be happy she was not here alone. That Seti was here too. The box came back to life as a male voice spoke, "Omari."

"What?" Doris retorted. "What does Om Ari mean?" They waited for a response.

Seti spoke up. "It is his name."

"His name?" Kaili gasped. Instantly Kaili shot a look to Doris. Doris was staring back. Kaili whispered "Someone else is here."

8

SAME DAY
NILE EGYPTIAN MUSEUM, FREMONT, CA

This new revelation had Kaili and Doris contemplating what this meant. Was there now a 3rd person? But Kaili had reviewed what Egyptian mummies the Museum had in storage. She was the one who encouraged the executives to invest in buying the bones she thought was the Queen of Egypt herself, Cleopatra.

As these thoughts swirled in Kaili's head, she went over to her computer to double check the inventory in storage again. This time she would do a broader search.

Doris came and looked over her shoulder to review the results with her. Kaili input the terms bone, skeleton, skull, mummy and hit enter. In a moment, the screen came to life with two results. One was that of an ancient animal from the 16th Dynasty. The other result was from a mummy found in Africa. Sudan to be exact.

Kaili looked over at Doris and whispered, "We have another one." As quickly as she could type, she entered in *Omari* into the search and hit return. The screen blinked and the results appeared: A common Sudanese male name.

Her breath left her lungs as she gasped.

"That would make sense," Doris retorted. "In 2014 a mummy of a woman was found in Sudan which was part of Egypt at one time. 2017 scientist performing DNA studies of Egyptian mummies found sub-Saharan African ancestry in post-Roman periods. It all fits. Due to Egypt's perfect location in Africa, international trade occurred very often between Africa, Asia, and Europe. There were foreign invaders as well."

Doris carried on, "Using radiocarbon dating Archaeologist have been able to break down discovered Mummies to 3 different time periods; Pre-Ptolemaic, Ptolemaic, and Roman periods."

Bells went off for Kaili. She knew that Selene was a relative of Ptolemy I Soter and Ptolemy II and that Selene was known as the African Queen.

Doing a little more research, Kaili found the information on where and when Omari's mummy was found. She jotted down the museum's codes and inventory location. She would need these.

While her mind was spinning with even more questions. Had Selene been speaking with him? Did she teach him about the spirit box?

"Omari, you are from Sudan?" Kaili asked. Tension mounted as they waited for a response. It was Selene. "Yes..."

Doris chimed in, "Are you Egyptian?" Selene again, "Partly ... part African."

Kaili knew immediately that she would have to acquire the bones from storage. She filled out the museum forms for permission and hand walked them to the Research Operations Office. She wanted this request rushed, but also recognized if she pushed too much, people would know something is up. That would be the last thing she needed.

Doris kept asking questions. "Selene you can speak with Omari, yes?"

"Yes"

It was getting a little more complicated but exhilarating all at the same time. What did this mean?

9

THAT NIGHT, AT THE WORTHY HOME COYOTE CREEK AREA OF SAN JOSE COUNTY, CA

By the time the ladies got back to the house, they were exhausted. Not knowing exactly what they had discovered that day, along with Derek's desire to not really talk about what he considered ghosts, they both found themselves somewhat silent.

Derek recognized the expression on their faces as being in a slight state of shock. Though they both greeted him as usual, it was definitely a contrived effort.

He had prepared his favorite stuffed green peppers and offer both of them dinner. Kaili and Doris realized they were hungrier than they expected. Kaili tried to force some conversation.

"How was your day dear?"

Thinking for a moment, Derek decided it was time to bring up the silence. "Well, my day was pretty normal. Not as exciting as yours I suspect."

Instantly Kaili knew her husband's detective skills were nothing to mess with. She decided she would go ahead and talk a little about the day's events.

"It seems like we have one more spirit at the museum. This time it is a mummy from Sudan." She paused for a moment to watch Derek's reaction. Slightly nodding his head up and down, Derek took in the information better than expected.

"This is getting larger by the day. Wondering if you have made these discoveries, why no one else has?"

Doris chimed in. "Maybe they have. And like us are afraid to make it public. This would shake the foundation of the world as we know it."

Derek and Kaili agreed.

"Or it was all Seti." Kaili exclaimed. "I mean...remember he has been at the museum for a long time. We hold classes on teaching Egyptian for beginners. He attended the classes, if I can call it that. He learned some English. How many other museums have this option?"

"That's a great point. My museum does not have those type of classes. Ours is more historical research." Doris thought out loud.

Observing the ladies, Derek noticed that they had relaxed a little after admitting to the day's activities. But true to form, he really didn't want to go into great detail. "What are your next steps?"

Glancing at Doris for her reaction, Kaili replied. "More questions tomorrow when we get in. Selene is interpreting for us. She ruled this area as part of her kingdom."

"It's time for bed," Derek almost demanded. Kaili had the haunting feeling that all was not right. Derek was not his happy self.

Clearing the dishes from the table, Doris offered to continue to clean up before going to bed.

Kaili and Derek said their good nights and went upstairs to their room. As soon as the bedroom door closed behind him, Derek started in.

"First know I trust Doris as much as you do. But this is going to blow up in your face. I cannot see this ending well at all."

It had been quite a while since Derek ever scolded her. He had reprimanded her once before when they were dating and Kaili had drank way too much.

She didn't like it then. And she wasn't thrilled about it now. But she knew he was right. Understanding Derek so much more now than back then, she appreciated his intent.

"I know. I'm scared." She looked up and met his eyes. "I don't know how this is going to turn out. I have no idea. But I also know," she hesitated, "I can't stop now. Not with what I know."

Slowly Derek walked over to her. He embraced her head into his hands. Then kissed her gently on the forehead. "I understand. We will deal with whatever comes our way…together."

Kaili tried to muster up a smile, but only got halfway. Derek leaned in, using his hands he pulled her to him and embraced Kaili in a full-on romantic kiss.

10

NEXT DAY
NILE EGYPTIAN MUSEUM, FREMONT, CA

Even with the cool morning air, the museum air condition was in full blast. The museum has to maintain certain temperatures in areas that housed artifacts.

This morning was bringing more tasks to Kaili as the mummy artifact she requested a couple of days ago was already sitting in her office. Doris was excited to see it as well. She picked up the plastic container that held the artifacts and brought it over to an empty table. Doris began to unwrap every piece from the safety wrapping and paper. Placing each body part gently onto the table.

As before with Selene's bones, Kaili wanted to extract DNA. She grabbed her tools and came over to where Doris was still unpacking everything. As she handled every bone, she could feel his soul. She could see that the knee bone showed wear of a particular pattern. As if the person walked with their knees always bent. A sign of aging or weakness or maybe a disease like malaria. Doris started to get a personal feeling of who Omari was and felt closer to him with each bone she touched.

Kaili was happy to see a molar on the jawbone. She easily loosens it and took it over to another open area in her office. Grabbing her drill, she worked on extracting material for the DNA Test.

As Doris finished placing every item from the container onto the table, she could see that the full mummy was not there. She checked the inventory list to verify her findings. The mummy was not whole. "Kaili, the full mummy is not here. The inventory says on it *When mummy was located, all body parts were not available.* At least we know no potential parts are misplaced."

"So hypothetically speaking part of Omari may still be at his burial location. Interesting." Not knowing what that could mean Kaili finished up placing the new DNA shavings into each container and prepped it for Carla to test. This time Kaili was in no rush to carry her samples to the lab herself. Using interoffice mail would be okay. She already knew who she was talking to in her office.

Placing the envelope in her out box, Kaili walked back over to the new mummy.

Kaili picked up the report that had accompanied the mummy.
"Report reads as follows: Located during 1912 exploration of surrounding area. North African; Sudan. Wadi Halfa (Gamai) near the border of Egypt; Nubian Desert / Lake Nassar area.

Preliminary findings: Male, age 32 to 39, North African descent, radiocarbon assay 9570 ± 64 years. Two sets of animal bones located in the same area also confirm radiocarbon dating as all are within 190 years.

The human excrement (coprolites) in the cave reveals, on the part of the ancient inhabitants, an incredibly coarse diet of seeds, hulls, and tough plant fibers. Analysis of the coprolites could not determine of the sex of the contributing individuals.

1995 study by Professor Alan Walter-Tilman extracted segments of mitochondrial DNA from Egyptian mummies. In 1999, undertaking a study, matches were made to this North African mummy by Geneticist Dr. Michael Sparks. No further studies undertaken. – End – "

Pictures of the mummy from original find still within the earth to its extraction from the site are included in the report.

"Where did you put the spirit box?" Doris asked. Kaili pointed to her top drawer of her desk. Doris pulled it out and hooked it up.

"Good morning everyone." Doris announced.

The box hissed as Seti replied, "hellooo" squeaked out.

"Is Omari with us? We have a mummy and skeleton we think is his? Can he confirm this?"

"Yes" Selene answered. "It is him."

"Nice to meet you." Doris greeted.

Selene continued to do her best to speak for Omari, but the translations still went through Seti since he could still speak English the best of the two. Often this would result in a slight delay from questions being posed and them actually answering Doris or Kaili.

The box buzzed again, and Selene began speaking, "He wants you to know they are still there."

Kaili was confused. Who was where? She inquired further. "Who is still there?" Seti jumped in. "His relatives are still there."

Well, that made sense. Most everyone has relatives

that died centuries ago. Kaili didn't think much of it. Maybe Omari wanted to reach out to them. "Do you want us to make contact for you? Return you to them?"

They waited for a response. Then Seti spoke. "Yes. It is important. Return me."

Doris found it interesting and asked Kaili a candid question, "Has either of them made this request?" Kaili shook her head no.

Kaili understood the request. If she, herself was ever taken from her grave, if she could, she would make the exact same request to be returned.

The spirit box cracked with Selene's voice, "It is very import-a-ant to him."

Compassion overwhelmed Kaili and Doris. But his mummy was a museum artifact. They would have to figure out a way to get the board members to agree.

"Maybe we can reach out to the representatives of the area to request the return of the mummy?" Doris blurted out.

Kaili thought out loud. "But they can't know it's us."

They both nodded in agreement.

11

NEXT NIGHT, AT THE WORTHY HOME COYOTE CREEK AREA OF SAN JOSE COUNTY, CA

A secret sadness was within Kaili as she pretended to be asleep that night. She has never kept any secrets from Derek and now felt that was all she was doing daily. There was so much she wanted to share with him but felt he would only tell her she was wrong. She valued his advice. Her brain was in full throttle trying to figure out how she was going to pull off her latest scheme.

Earlier that day, Kaili had located 2 museums near where Omari's mummy was discovered. She drafted letters and sent them via a local fax office, at an internet café, to the Museum in Wadi Halfa and one in Gamai. Both letters were sent anonymously as Kaili was very aware the executives at the Nile Egyptian Museum would not be happy.

Not moving and trying very hard to make sure she would not wake Derek sleeping next to her, Kaili had to fight the urge to move around like she normally does when she is restless. Derek would always awake on those nights knowing something was bothering her. She did not want to have to explain her actions. Being married to a Police Officer had its advantages and also had its drawbacks when you are trying to hide something.

She wondered if there would be any reaction to her letters. Would either museum want to have the mummy returned to its homeland? Would they respect the mummy and bury it again? Or was she just making matters worse, and Omari would end up on display in their museum instead.

Kaili knew she couldn't tell the Sudan authorities what she knew and why. Somehow, she would have to try to persuade them to return the mummy to the burial origins. She had no idea how she will do that if they insist on keeping Omari in the museum.

Questioning herself, Kaili worried that maybe she acted too hurriedly and maybe did not think it through. Would he be better off where he could communicate with Seti and Selene? Omari's request came off as desperate, that of a great need. How did she really know that? Other than the first time being able to speak it was a top request. Selene and Seti had actually interpreted the conversation for her. Therefore, Kaili was not completely assured of how essential it was for Omari to return home.

Kaili decided she would let them know tomorrow morning. She would explain what she had done and what the possible outcomes could be. She knew she could be worrying about nothing at all. She had no way of knowing if the Museum's even cared. It was apparent they had never tried to obtain the Mummy back before now.

If only she could get her mind to settle down, she could get some sleep. It was going to be a long night.

What Kaili didn't fully factor in was that it was already 10 am in Sudan and the two museum executives were talking to each other. They were excited to have this new information and would be reaching out as soon as the Nile Egyptian Museum opened in the morning.

12

THE FOLLOWING DAY
NILE EGYPTIAN MUSEUM, FREMONT, CA

Even before Kaili and Doris could return to the office, the museum was buzzing. Sudanese officials had already reached out to the museum executives. They wanted to work out a deal to return the mummy to its motherland. But they wanted one more thing. They sought to make it an international thank you for respecting both the mummy and their heritage.

The Nile Egyptian Museum thought it was a great way to strengthen communication with that region of the world. They felt the Sudan Mummy would yield little to their museum compared to mummies located further north in Egypt.

As the ladies arrived at the office there was an entourage of people awaiting them. Pretending to be unaware of the request, Kaili had to use her best acting skills as she walked in through the front door. Kaili really didn't know if the situation was bad or good. Had they found out she sent the letters?

"Morning Dr. Worthy, Dr. Wolf."

"Morning" Kaili replied.

"We have a terrific opportunity to forge a relationship with the Sudanese Government, and we will need your assistance." Said one of the executives.

Not wanting to take anyone into her office right now knowing the circumstances, she made a suggestion, "If we could go talk somewhere, I would be happy to discuss."

Off to the left of the Museum entrance was a large meeting room which would be perfect. The executives lead the way while Kaili and Doris followed. Everyone took their seats while Kaili placed her purse and coat on the seat next to her. She took a chair directly across from the head executive. Doris sat to her right.

Doris knew it would be best if she didn't speak right now. She knew of the letters that Kaili had sent the night before and recognized the fact that Kaili had no intention of divulging the information to anyone, especially Museum Executives.

The Executive continued to lead the discussion. "We want to return the Sudan Mummy to its original location where it was discovered. We have an official government request to do so. We all think that honoring that request would be a fantastic gesture to both Sudan and Egyptian authorities."

Kaili was excited to hear the news. She wondered exactly what was meant when they said they wanted to return the mummy to its original resting place. She had only hoped they meant more than just his country but his actual burial spot. That would be the best based on Omari's request. There would be one way she would know for sure.

"I think we have all the information we can gleam off of the mummy. As you know his DNA revealed he has Egyptian ancestry, which does make sense." She paused and then made her own request, "We would like to accompany the mummy back to Sudan."

Doris caught that. Who was 'we'? Kaili had not said a thing to her about going to the African continent. Doris knew she had become an essential part of the new discovery and already knew what Kaili was thinking. They had been friends so long that this was more common occurrence between the two than probably most. Doris knew she would dare not show her confusion in her face at this moment. She simply nodded yes accordingly.

The executive looked at all the others, with each one of them shaking their head in agreement. "Great. We were hoping you would ask. We want you to represent us especially since you are familiar with the mummy in question. You can share your findings with them."

Kaili stood up at the same time as the Executive did and reached out to shake his hand in agreement. Kaili moved slowly gathering up her purse and coat as the executives left the room. As soon as the door closed Doris raised the obvious question? "We? Who is we?"

Kaili turned around and shot Doris a huge smile. "You know that answer."

"Well, Sudan here we come."

That night Kaili informed Derek of the Museum's suggestion and that she and Doris had accepted the request to accompany the mummy home.

Derek thought it was a great idea. It made a lot of sense to him. Though he never liked Kaili traveling without him, this time it would be a much shorter trip than the last one.

13

THE NEXT WEEK
KHARTOUM. SUDAN

The 19 plus hours felt like they must have flown around the world twice. Doris could easily sleep while Kaili just never felt comfortable. Kaili was always afraid she would start snoring loudly and disturb the other passengers.

They had both brought their own blankets and sleep pillows making the flight a bit more comfortable. In addition, Doris always brought great snacks along on any trip they ever took. Kaili bought several bottles of water for the both of them.

The flight allowed time to do more research on the area Omari mummy was located. They also played some on-line games to help pass the time. They were constantly laughing at something.

The whole affair seems so sudden. Kaili had hoped to be able to run the DNA through a genealogy website to see if they could locate any living relatives to attend the reburial ceremony. Knowing the souls followed their remains was still a heavy burden to carry for her.

As the plane finally landed at the Khartoum Sudan International Airport, they were both ready to stretch their legs and walk at little. Kaili and Doris grabbed a couple of additional clothing items to ensure their appearance would not offend anyone meeting them at the plane. They ensured their shoulders were covered and both had worn long pleaded skirts that went below their knees.

As the plane unloaded Kaili and Doris were met at the gate by Sudan dignitaries. Greetings and introductions were exchanged. The Security team helped to carry their luggage and loaded into an all-black SUV with tinted windows. There were two other Government SUVs and a hearse in the group.

Kaili was incredibly happy to see the luggage had made the trip unscathed. As she had cleverly packed away Selene and Seti's bones among her articles. She knew she might need them if Omari wanted to reach out.

As they started to head out, they found themselves circling back behind the airport. There they saw a casket being unloaded from the plane. Kaili and Doris felt the need to get out of the car to pay tribute to the coffin as it was carried to the hearse. Once loaded in the hearse, everyone got back in the cars and headed out to their destination.

As they arrived at the Sudan International Hotel, Kaili and Doris knew that sleep would have to wait as the ceremony rehearsal information would be provided that very afternoon to ready them for the following days.

Quickly they were ushered to a large conference room where several well-dressed men were sitting. As they entered the men stood up to greet them. Each man expressed their appreciation for the mummy's return.

A light lunch was offered and served. A gesture of

friendship. The men sat together, and though it appeared to be one table, due to the tablecloth, the women sat at another. All items were placed at the center area of the table. The host began to present each dish to the guests which, after serving themselves, Kaili and Doris passed to their right as is the custom. Kaili was delighted in seeing several of her favorite Mediterranean dishes. Hummus was always one of Kaili's favorites. The meal also included red lentil soup and fresh bread. And a salad of tomatoes, diced cucumbers, spring onions, mixed with peanut butter and lemon juice. It was very refreshing.

After social visiting, asking about families and recent discoveries, the conversation turned to the details of the reburial. The discussion started by talking about who would be in attendance, along with what would be expected of both Kaili and Doris during the ceremony. They would be given an honor of making an offering at the site if they chose to do so. It would be disrespectful if they decline. But Kaili felt it was an exceptional offer since they had spoken with Omari already. It would be an early morning since the drive from Khartoum to Wadi Halfa, Sudan would be just over 12 hours.

Rising early the next morning, they both dressed appropriately for traveling in a car for some time, and to be respectful of all customs. Both had been to this region before. They knew that scarfs were essential part of the outfit due to the sand and dust filled air. Walking shoes would be required. Though Doris would prefer on-trail hiking boots, they knew they may visit someone's home once arriving. Hiking boots are more difficult to remove and put back on when entering and leaving a home in Sudan.

The train that ran along the Nile from Khartoum and further had long since stopped running which would have shorten the travel time. But that did not bother either of the ladies. In their opinion, the train passed by everything too fast.

As they rode in the luxury SUV, they both took in the rolling hills of golden-brown sand. The tops of the hills appeared as if they were burnt from the sun as darker sand shown there. The wind left ripple marks in the sand in some areas. In other places rock poked out of the sand as if to try to claim its stake in the land. Little townships of clay buildings would pop-up from time to time along the route.

Periodically a bus stuffed with passengers inside and with people jammed on top of it was driving in the opposite direction. It would be so packed with passengers, it was scary. Since there are not a lot of options for those needing to make the trip, buses are a common mode of transportation. Doris almost felt guilty having a nice airconditioned SUV to be sitting in not to mention the nice bucket style seats.

The cars all stopped as they came upon a small outpost. Outside a small clay building there was a table set up with several items of food. The bowls of beans and Kisra (flatbread) were offered. Though the dignitaries had brought a lunch with them for everyone, they offered a rest and the taste of authentic home cooking.

Again, Doris and Kaili found themselves being very appreciative. There was no rush to arrive in Khartoum before mid-day anyways. Meeting the people of the land was a fond love of Kaili's. They seemed to always be a happy people. They loved to meet others as well. Americans could mean good money, if they were first time tourists. But Kaili and Doris were not. Both were well aware of what items costs in the land. It didn't matter since their entourage paid for the meal. The escort also made sure that nothing would be happening to the ladies. They were going to make sure of that.

14

THE NEXT DAY
KHARTOUM, SUDAN

The sun rose over the sand dunes it painted the sand a golden color on one side, casting a dark black shadow in the other. Every wind formed ripple is highlighted in the same way. If not for the gilded sand color, one might think they were looking at the ocean with rippled waves.

As the sun hung like an ornament in the sky, going higher and higher, the shadows began to disappear and the barrenness of the land reappeared.

They traded in their plush SUVs to open-air modified 4-wheel drive jeeps for transporting the party through the sand. The big tires that are slightly deflated allowing the jeep to feel like it was floating on the sand, instead of digging into it. As they headed out it in a long single file line of vehicles it was apparent, they would be traveling at a much slower speed as they carefully approached the top of every dune before going over it. No wild rollercoaster style driving today.

Some rocky hills were just on their horizon. They seemed to be heading straight for them. There wasn't a lot of discussion going on due to the fact that the tires constantly kicked up some sand.

As they moved towards the hills, they began to feel

as if they loomed over them. Kaili instinctively grabbed the Jeep's role bar even though they were tucked in with harness style seat belts.

The driver attacked the hill straight on, moving at a slow pace keeping all four tires on the ground as much as possible. As they reached the crest of the hill, the driver slowed to a stop. As the driver stepped out of the Jeep to scan the backside of the hill and determine the best way down, Kaili and Doris could see their destination.

There in the city below them appeared to be a circular city built into the ground. There was a definite center of town, with buildings and dwelling assembled to face the center of the archaeological site. Several pillars were still standing erect as if there was a ceiling at one time.

The site reminded Doris of the ruins of Göbekli Tepe in Turkey. The big difference here is that the site below them is that it was also carved into the hillside on the opposite side of the small valley.

Within moments the driver was back in the jeep, and they were all heading downhill rocking a little bit back and forth as they navigated the rocky terrain.

Kaili and Doris could hardly contain themselves as they got closer and closer to their destination. Omari was almost home.

Arriving at their journey's end, Kaili and Doris popped out of the vehicle they had been riding in and walked rapidly to the edge of the site. There they took in the dusty smells and design. Kaili immediately spoke of the obvious. "This reminds me of Göbekli Tepe, one of the oldest temples ever discovered." Doris could not agree more. "But instead of just it being a temple, it appears to be a city that was underground. Or built to resemble as being under the earth.

Kaili pulled out the speaker box and made sure they were a good distance from the rest of the team members. She switched it on. Doris looked concerned, but at the same time the excitement welled up in her.

"Omari are you here?" they paused for the response.

"With my people" came from Selene.

Kaili and Doris wanted to scream with excitement but knew better. It had worked. Kaili was carrying Seti's and Selene's small remains with her. It was fortuitous that this plan would work at all. The pleasant unexpected results were very exhilarating.

"You will be back home shortly Omari," Kaili spoke slowly and clearly.

"With my people" was the repeated response.

The other team members were beginning to approach. Kaili didn't get to say anything more for now.

The dignitaries' shuffled out of their jeeps as the casket was brought forward. One of the guides pointed out the area where the remains of Omari had originally been located. The plan was to return the remains to the same location and seal off the entrance. Markers had been created to denote the tomb with the information they had learned about the leader.

Everyone was led down into the city and into an open passageway. The climb down was steep, the team moved slowly. The passageway was one of several excavated a few years earlier. It was pitch black inside. Bright battery-operated lights had been brought in and set up the night before.

The party entered the passageway. The cold stone walls let the temperature drop at least 15 degrees. As they ventured in further, it got cooler and cooler. In addition, carving began to appear on the walls. These carvings were very Egyptian in nature. Animals and war scenes were displayed. The carvings were also painted to accent them all.

Kaili and Doris could now see a huge opening in the passage way ahead. Before entering one could see two columns carved into the stone as if you were entering a temple. The square chamber had a rectangular hole in the center of it. The large cavern tomb was around 14 feet by 16 feet and only 6 feet high. Kaili or Doris could easily touch the ceiling.

When the find was originally opened the room had been filled with woven baskets of dry food, a carved boat, carved animals, clay pots with organs or oils. All of these items had been removed.

As they began the ceremony almost immediately, each dignitary carried an item with them. They made offerings of the dry food, oils, and carvings of the animals and the boat. Kaili and Doris offered up incense and lit the fragrance fill the chamber as the work crew placed the remains in a newly painted replica sarcophagus and then was lowered down.

The area was filled in. Some sacred oils were sprinkled over the new dirt and large stone slabs were laid over the burial place. People started to leave, exiting through the same passage way they had entered.

Several jeeps filled up and left the location. Kaili and Doris wanted to watch the tomb be officially closed. In addition, they have been given permission to linger a little longer to study the city and excavation site.

15

EARLY EVENING OF THE SAME DAY
KHARTOUM, SUDAN

Only two jeeps remained. One was Kaili and Doris's and the other was for the workers who were adding the marker to the stone granite closure they put to seal the tomb. They were just about finished.

Kaili and Doris had already started to survey the city. Doris was taking pictures off all the carvings and painting she could. Kaili began looking into the other passageways that had been unearthed years ago. Her halogen flashlight lit up the passage way pretty well as the glow surrounded her. She wondered if they were fake entrances to other rooms to discourage finding the real tomb or if they were openings to other tombs. She didn't want to venture too far in as she was entering alone. Going into caves or tunnels alone is never a safe move.

As she explored the second passageway Kaili pulled out the spirit box again. Could Omari still hear her? Clicking in on, static filled the air and bounced off the walls. Kaili immediately turned the volume down. "Omari, can you still hear me?"

"Yes."

His spirit was dwelling in the structure. He was here. Before she asked the next question, the spirit box came alive. Seti's voice was heard speaking for Omari. "My people thank you. You are honorable"

Kaili wasn't sure what to make of the statement. "You are welcome."

Suddenly Doris was right behind Kaili. A sand storm had kicked up and they would have to wait it out. The Jeep driver had already jumped into another passage way closer to the vehicle. Hopefully, it would pass as quickly as it showed up.

This would give Kaili and Doris more time to use the spirit box and communicate with Omari.

They walked in a little further and saw no end in sight. Kaili had hoped they would find a chamber like the one Omari was buried in to wait out the storm.

After walking another 100 feet, Kaili stopped and turned to Doris. "Not sure we should keep walking. I see nothing different ahead." Without the proper equipment and not knowing what was taking place outside, Doris agreed.

They both leaned against the wall and slipped down to the floor to have a seat. Kaili let Doris know they could still speak with Omari through Seti and Selene, just as they had done in her office days earlier.

Doris jumped at the chance. "Omari, was this city underground or a built temple?" The air was silent. Kaili thought she would try different wording in case they did not understand. "Was the city below the surface? Under the dirt?"

A crackle was heard followed by "lived in the earth."

Doris continued. "Do you know where we are right now?"

The speaker lit up. "Yes. Near my people."

Doris wanted to know if they venture ahead would they find another tomb maybe?

The spirit box was quiet. Then Selene spoke "You would find many."

Many tombs Doris' thought. That would be an amazing find. Kaili had concerns. "I am not sure us locating more tombs is a good thing." Doris understood Kaili's concerns. The place would become infected with archaeologist trying to make a name for themselves. They would have even more souls unearthed. Knowing this was becoming a heavier burden to carry every day.

This would be a great time to bounce the idea off her husband. Go forward and see what they see. Or just leave it. Let the souls rest in peace.

As they both silently contemplated their next actions, a light from farther down the tunnel was heading towards them. The driver must have found his way around the tunnels to get to them. Kaili quickly ensured the spirit box was turned off and stowed it into her jacket pocket.

As the light slowly approached them the glow seemed different. It wasn't as bright as her flashlight. Maybe the driver had an older version. Halogens can be pretty blinding when approaching others.

Doris felt a bit of comfort knowing the driver would be with them. Maybe he was going to let them know the storm was over. Good thing was that they would have two exits in case one was blocked by the sand.

Shuffling sounds started to echo off the tunnel walls. Kaili had always had a pet peeve about people not picking up their feet. She found the sound annoying. Beggars can't be choosers she said to herself as her hero was forthcoming.

Doris tapped Kaili's shoulder to look down the tunnel. It wasn't a flashlight at all. It was some kind of lantern. Kaili strained her eyes to try to see better. She could swear the driver was not alone.

Who else was there? Did the workers join him when the storm hit?

The light was only yards away now. They could both hear the people speaking to each other but neither of them could make out the language.

The realization this was not the driver, or the other workers hit Kaili and Doris at the same time. It is Omari's people.

Doris let out a gasp. There were no words. Their brains scrambled to make sense of it all. How could it be? Both slowly stood up as they faced about 20 people carrying ancient style lanterns. The leader of the group was a young man who offered his hand to Kaili to get her to follow him. He began to lead her and Doris deeper into the mountain. She could feel the ground lowering them further into the earth.

They came around a corner and saw a huge cavern full of different people. She tried to count but gave up. There were probably a good 100 individuals living in the mountain. There were several out coves and additional little openings that people filled. Kaili could only suspect they were family units. Men, women, and children. A few small animals and what appeared to be a small freshwater stream cutting its way through the mountain.

The people stood no taller than five-feet. Most were under four and a half feet tall. Probably due to living underground. Their skin, though a little dirty, showed no signs of sunlight tanning. Most of the people had very white or light skin.

Pottery or shaved rocks were used as utensils and cooking devices. The lights they used to find her, were of some kind of oil base that did not create soot and seemed to burn gradually and not quickly. Hand woven blankets and some animal furs lined the floors.

Catching up with her thoughts as she took in all the sites, Kaili knew this was an undiscovered civilization. This discovery would change the world. This discovery would destroy theirs.

Doris grabbed Kaili's arm. "The spirit box."

"What about it?"

"Omari can speak with his people."

Doris was brilliant, Kaili thought. She wasn't sure if the ancient people would understand how the spirit box worked or what was going on, but she knew they had to give it a try.

Kaili pulled it out of her pocket and clicked it on. The spirit box crackled with a fiery start. Omari began to speak directly to his people. Gasps came from many of the people as they began to carefully approach and surround Kaili and Doris. Omari continued to speak in their language. Kaili and Doris could only make out a few words. "Returned me," "Family," and "Souls." Omari stopped speaking. Selene began to translate. "These are the people who brought me back to you. They are part of our family. They have our souls within them. Welcome them."

Kaili wanted to cry as the crowd began to chant. She and Doris knew they were not worthy off all the praise being bestowed on them. They knew their very presence was putting every person there in jeopardy.

Kaili wanted to tell them that the only thing they did was bring Omari back. They understood the significance of returning a king to his people, but nothing is ever that simple.

Doris knew they could not stay. In fact, she feared if the driver was coming to find them, they would find the people. "We have to go." Doris warned Kaili. Kaili knew she was right.

16

SUDAN EXCAVATION SITE, SAME DAY
KHARTOUM, SUDAN

The young male leader of the group understood Kaili's gesture about having to leave. It seemed to both Kaili and Doris that the leader understood they could not be missing for long or his people would be discovered.

He and a couple of men helped start to escort the ladies back to their original location in the tunnel. When they got back to the corner that hid the cavern, two of the men moved a large rock as to close it off and create a dead end to the tunnel. No wonder why they had never been discovered.

They lead Kaili and Doris back to the same spot they had found them earlier. The spirit box in her pocket was still turned on. Omari spoke. His voice shocked them all. Kaili's heart jumped as she first thought it was their driver and they had all been discovered. Just as fast, she realized it was Omari and she had not turned the box off. The 2 men bowed to Kaili and Doris. Kaili and Doris responded by bowing to the men.

Selene spoke "You are honorable. Save my people." Kaili swallowed hard. She knew that meant they would have to keep this secret and take it to their own graves.

With that the men turned and disappeared within the tunnel darkness.

Kaili looked at Doris. "We can't say anything" paused "Ever." Doris nodded yes. She understood all of the implications.

They started to head back out the tunnel the way they came in. Both in shock, they walked back in complete silence. Reflecting on the day's events they worried that somehow others would know what happened.

A few yards from the entrance they found their driver waiting. "The storm has passed. We can head home."

Kaili could hardly speak and mustered out a faint "Okay. Let's go."

Hardly a word was spoken on the entire trip home. Overwhelmed with astonishment at their find and all the consequences this discover could entail affected everything they were now a part of.

A secret that could never, ever be shared. A place they should never return to.

The expression on the faces of Kaili and Doris appeared as if a big rig truck had hit them. Stone faces full of concern and guilt mixed with excitement.

Kaili was overly concerned that her husband was going to know something is very, very wrong the moment he lays eyes on her. How could she keep this secret from him? He would interrogate her until she confessed. After all that was his job, and he was good at it.

Could he? Would he? Keep her secret? He knew her too well to know if she was lying or if it was the truth. That wasn't her concern. He would believe her. She knew she would have to trust him. Revealing how this took place, the letter she sent, the finding of the civilization she cannot talk about, and everything in between was going to be a judgement she did not want to face with her husband, but she knew arriving home was going to be a long night. And not the welcome home night she would prefer to have.

She stepped off the plane in San Francisco. Her heart was beating rapidly. So much to confess. Why did she marry a police captain? She thought.

Maybe the better question could be "Why is she so mischievous?"

There he was. Derek standing there to welcome her home, but his expression changed quickly as he saw her face. He knew the look well.

EPILOGUE

After getting Doris on her next flight to return home, Kaili and Derek headed to their car in silence. Derek knew very well that Kaili would be confessing to something. He just didn't know what. He remembered the day they met. It literally set the tone for their entire relationship.

Derek was on duty as a sergeant back then and was on patrol that late night. Someone called in to the station and reported teenagers defacing a hillside with graffiti. As he and his partner Mike arrived at the scene, he found four adults chiseling away at the mountain side.

As Derek approached the group he asked "Excuse me. What are you all doing?" One member of the group turned around and told Officer Worthy that they were digging for artifacts and that they were all graduates in archaeology. That was Derek's first clue they were probably drunk. It was the first time he laid eyes on Kaili. Kaili and Doris were still picking at the hillside and giggling. It seemed they were finding some seashells and other ocean bottom fossils.

Kaili was certainly dressed up for a night out. Her dark hair was down. She wore a somewhat tight pink sweater and tight black leather pants. Derek noted her heels certainly were not the right shoes to be wearing on a dig. He found her laughter was contagious.

Derek sharply asked, "Have you all been drinking?"

That stopped Kaili and Doris who then turned around. They sheepishly looked at the handsome officer in his uniform. Robert, the fourth member of the digging team spoke up, "I am the designated driver." Pointing at their car, Derek asked "Is this your car?" Robert replied yes.

Wanting to know a little more about Kaili, Derek didn't want to see her go quite yet, he came up with a plan. Derek barked out some orders, "Turn and face the car. Hands on the car." He paused for a second. "Now!!" He wanted to add a little fear to the situation. He told his partner Mike to take the first two. That left Kaili and Robert for Derek.

Derek approached Kaili and pushed her arms up a little higher. Then he started to pat her down. She began to wiggle and laugh. "Ma'am you need to stop moving." He commanded. Kaili stopped. "You're tickling me." Derek knew that wasn't true. Patting someone down never tickled. He decided to pat her down a little harder. There would be no way he is tickling her now. He began again. Yet she still giggled and moved like he was still tickling her. Derek knew instantly it was a put on. He wasn't 100% sure what came over him, but he took his hand and smacked her on her bottom. Kaili took notice and submitted immediately.

Once everyone was frisked and found okay, Derek ordered them all to turn around and face him. He then asked for everyone's ID. Everyone complied. Mike checked the first two again while Derek started to memorize Kaili's name and address. Derek was known for his photographic memory. Once they were done, he told them to leave.

Robert got in the driver's seat, and they left. Derek and Mike went back into the vehicle. Mike looked at Derek and couldn't help asking, "What was that?" Derek laughed a little. Mike continued, "She is cute."

The next morning Derek showed up at Kaili's house. He wanted to make sure she was all right. He knocked on her door and she answered. She recognized him immediately, even in his civilian clothes. She invited him in and offered him some coffee. "Cream or sugar?"

"Yes, Cream. Thanks." She brought the coffee over, and they both sat at her kitchen table. "I wanted to make sure you were okay." Kaili raised one eyebrow in question. "Really? You do this to all your jailbirds? Come by and visit?" Calling his bluff. She knew why he was there and she was just as happy to see him. She continued as she witnesses Derek's face expression change as he realized that his ruse did not work for a second. "I need to say two things. One, I apologize for the way I acted last night. It doesn't take much alcohol to make me frisky." Derek immediately took that information in and filed it away. Since then, he has used that information repeatedly.

Derek pushed her on "Apology accepted. And two?"

"You." She replied. "I am fairly sure that spanking a person in your custody is not permitted in your rule book. What would your captain say if she or he found out?"

That's the very moment Derek knew he wanted her. She was smart, intelligent, feisty, and gorgeous. He swallowed hard as he knew she was not through yet.

"Ever hear the phrase turnabout is fair play?" That sinched it for him. Playful too and not afraid to take back the reigns. He was not going to let her go.

Derek never forgot a single detail of that first meeting. He reminisced as they headed home. Derek knew he would have to start the conversation this time. "Well, my week was interesting. Thanks for asking. There was a burglary gang we broke up. One hit and run car accident solved. And A few minor disturbances."

Kaili realized she had been bad company for the ride home but was thankful they would be home shortly. Once there Derek took her bags in and up to their room. As he came back down the stairs, he saw Kaili sitting on the couch with her head in her hands. Obviously conflicted.

He went over and poured her some wine, knowing it would loosen her up. He got himself a beer so the move of giving her alcohol would not stand out as much.

Kaili thanked him and began to drink the wine. Derek positioned himself in the big chair directly across from her instead of sitting on the couch next to her. A great interview tactic. He just sat there looking at her. No questions. No big movements. He knew that ploy made people uneasy. He felt a little guilty using his training on her, but he was also enjoying her squirming a little.

Kaili began to confess. She told him about the Spirit Box and how a third voice came through. She went on to say she found another mummy in the museums archive and gathered the fossils to her office. She told him how Selene and Seti could help interpret what the new soul was saying because Cleopatra Selene had ruled over the region where his mummy was excavated.

Derek was taking it all in. Listening and noting

everything. Kaili continued and told Derek about the request Omari had made to return his body back to his homeland. How conflicted she felt that a soul had been unearthed and disturbed. She admitted to sending the anonymous letters to the Sudanese officials.

Derek took a sip of his beer, but continued in silence, listening to every word. Kaili glanced at him to see if she could read him. But like a great detective, Derek was stoned faced.

She continued talking as she wanted it all out in the open. She couldn't tell him fast enough. She wanted all the information exposed.

Kaili went on about how she suggested she should travel with the remains, how they brought the spirit box with them and about the excavation site and reburial ceremony. She stopped to take in a deep breath before divulging the rest.

She began to explain the trip in the tunnel, the lantern coming towards them and the people living there. Derek was intrigued.

She spoke about her and Doris's decision to leave the people be. How they were concerned that their discovery to the world would destroy everything.

Then she stopped and waited for Derek to say something. She used the opportunity to finish her wine.

He sat up in the chair and could only mutter "Wow." He was still getting his head wrapped around all the information. After a minute He spoke up again. "That is amazing. I am so proud of you." Kaili looked up and locked eyes. She could see the pride in his face and smile. "That is probably the most humane thing you could do. Kaili you are right. The people have been hidden until now and need to stay that way. That is a big secret to keep."

"I know. I trust you so much and know I couldn't keep it from you. Sorry to burden you with it."

"No burden dear. I have to keep secrets for a living."

He stood up and went over to her. She stood to meet him face to face. He gave her a huge hug and held on for a bit. He could see the relief in her face. It was all out in the open now. But Derek knew there was still one thing not finished yet that he could use to his advantage.

"Thank you for telling me all about this. We promised to never keep anything from each other."

Moving back slightly from their embrace, Derek put his hands on each of Kaili's shoulders. "Well young lady there is only one more thing to do." He stated. "Time for you to go up to bed and wait for me."

Kaili thought that was an odd thing to say. "Wait for you?" she questioned.

Derek smirked. "There is that issued of the anonymous letters you sent out. I am fairly sure the Museum Executives would not be pleased with you going rogue."

Kaili had hoped Derek had not picked up on that part of the story. Her plan was that the discovery of the people was supposed to be so overwhelming it would become his focus. Who was she kidding?

Instantly she became somewhat submissive. She knew Derek was going to use this incident to his advantage. Then again, did she care?? Not really.

"Now go upstairs. I will be up in a minute. Think

about what you did" he said in a playful lecturing tone. As she turned to go up the stairs, he lightly patted her bottom as a message of what was to come.

He gathered the wine glass and beer bottle and took them to the kitchen sink. To stall a little longer, he took time to wash and dry the wine glass. As he deliberately walked toward the stairs, he switched off the lights along the way. Just before ascending up the staircase to their room, a huge smile came across his face. This was going to be fun. It brought back those old memories. He was happy that the two of them were still as playful as ever.

ABOUT THE AUTHOR

Kay has worked in the entertainment industry for many years from editing to writing and even producing.

Her passion is in creating intelligent entertainment for everyone to enjoy. She holds an MBA, and a few certificates. Her first book was developed from her thesis about the prevention of workplace violence - a non-fiction book. Now her collection of Fiction books is a way to combine her passion for writing and archaeology.

Her hobbies include learning about new archaeological finds, science, and history. Her writing includes previous books, writing for TV and films, and motivational shorts.

Made in the USA
Coppell, TX
24 July 2021

59425110R00046